BEAT THE MACKERS

Stephanie Dagg

MENTOR
BOOKS

This Edition first published 2001 by

MENTOR BOOKS
43 Furze Road,
Sandyford Industrial Estate,
Dublin 18.

Tel. + 353 1 295 2112/3   Fax. +353 1 295 2114
e-mail: admin@mentorbooks.ie
www.mentorbooks.ie

ISBN: 1-84210-073-4

A catalogue record for this book is available
from the British Library

Cover Illustration: Jimmy Lawlor
Typesetting, editing, design and layout by
MENTOR BOOKS
Printed in Ireland by Colour Books
1 3 5 7 9 10 8 6 4 2

Contents

The Author

Stephanie Dagg

Stephanie Dagg lives in Innishannon, Co.Cork, with husband Chris and children Benjamin and Caitlín.

She has been writing stories ever since she was a child in Suffolk in England. As well as writing, Stephanie works as an editor. In her spare time she loves swimming, cycling, gardening and walking her two dogs. She's also very interested in computers and the Internet. Check out her website at www.booksarecool.net.

To Lieut. Jim Oakley

17.2.1919 — 28.9.2000

Thanks for everything, Dad.

Monday 13 January 2003

Heather Mayhew trudged up the steep hill towards her house. She'd just got off the bus from school. Now that she was twelve, her father said she could walk home on her own. But even though he didn't come down the road to meet her any more, Heather knew he'd be watching the clock carefully, and if she was more than a few minutes late he'd be out looking for her.

Ray Mayhew ran his computer programming business from home. And what a home it was! He and Heather lived in a huge, rambling house surrounded by several acres of garden and orchards. Ray's business was extremely successful these days. He'd had a big breakthrough when he'd developed an anti-millennium bug program back in 1998. It had been the first, and best, compliance-testing software on the market and he'd made a lot of money from it. So Heather had everything she could possibly need – and a few more things besides. She didn't think herself particularly lucky though. She just took it for granted.

'Hi Dad!' called Heather as she opened the front door.

'Hi love!' shouted Ray from his office at the top of the stairs. 'I'll be down in a sec. Pop the kettle on please, will you?'

Heather and her father always had a cup of tea together when she got back from school. Then Heather would get on with her homework and Ray would go back to his office upstairs, except for Tuesdays when they went swimming and Fridays when Heather went to ballet. But today was Monday so Heather had the evening to herself. She decided she'd get her roller skates out later since it was a warm, bright day. And then maybe she'd watch television or read. She hummed happily as she filled the kettle up. She was very content with her ordered, steady life.

A clumping on the stairs signalled that her father was coming down. She pulled the biscuit barrel out of the cupboard and put some of his favourite digestives on a plate. She fished out some ginger nuts for herself.

'So what did you learn today, princess?' smiled Ray as he came into the kitchen. He was small and wiry, with unfashionable thick, black-framed glasses, a bushy beard and a lot of ginger hair. He was usually very scruffy, except for when he met clients. Today was not a day of meetings so he was dressed in baggy jogging pants, a shabby checked shirt and odd slippers. But Heather didn't notice. Her father always looked something like that.

'Oh, we did loads of stuff today,' she replied. 'We're reading a great book at the moment, all about some lady explorer. I can't remember her name though.

How's your new program going?'

'Fine, fine,' smiled Ray. 'Not too much more to do on it now.'

'It's an anti-hacking program, right?' said Heather conversationally, dunking two ginger nuts at once into her sweet, milky tea.

'It certainly is,' he nodded, adding a fourth spoonful of sugar to his mug of black tea. Neither passed a comment on the other's behaviour, or even noticed it.

'So, you'll stop all these nasty hackers messing up other people's computers just for fun, right?' said Heather. 'Good for you, Dad.'

She munched her biscuit thoughtfully. 'But why do hackers do what they do?' she demanded.

Ray shrugged. 'Like you said, they're plain nasty people. Well, most of them are. Some are harmless enough.'

'They don't *sound* harmless,' protested Heather.

'What I mean,' he went on, 'is that some hackers break into systems just to see if they can. They leave a message describing what they've done so that the person at the other end can tighten up on security before a malicious hacker, or cracker, gets in the same way.'

'Still sneaky,' observed Heather. 'And why is there so much hacking these days? I mean, a few years ago there didn't seem to be much going on, but now there's loads.'

Heather was right. In the last two days alone, a thirteen-year-old girl in America had crippled three huge corporations by hacking into their websites. And in Luxembourg the computer systems of the European Union had been sabotaged by some as yet unknown hackers.

'It's easier these days, Heth,' her father sighed. 'Mainly because of cable modems.'

Heather helped herself to a few more ginger nuts. 'Cable modems?' she echoed. 'I know what modems are. They're what link a computer to the telephone system so it can go online, aren't they? Do cable modems link to cable TV or something?'

Ray smiled. 'They can do, but usually they're independent. What they are is this. With a cable modem a computer is linked to the Internet continuously. And it doesn't tie up the telephone line either. Now, we have a dial-up connection. When we want to go online, we have to tell the computer to hook up – and we can't use the phone in the meantime. But the advantage of a dial-up connection is that it is a limited link up to the Internet. And that makes it harder for a hacker to track us down because we're not always there. However, cable modems mean a computer has a static address that's there all day, every day . . .'

'Twenty-four seven, you mean,' Heather corrected him. 'That's the cool way to say it!'

'OK, twenty-four seven,' Ray agreed, picking up

three more digestives. 'So it's easier for a hacker browsing around to find an address to attack.'

'What do you mean by address? Do you mean the website name?' Heather was puzzled.

'No, I actually mean the IP address – the Internet Protocol address.' Seeing his daughter's frown, he quickly went on. 'Each computer on the Internet has a unique IP address, which is a series of numbers in groups of three. These numbers are the way information finds its way from the source to where it's going. The website names, or domain names, aren't what the computers actually use. They're just there for the humans! People are better at remembering names than series of numbers. Although that might change in a few thousand years' time,' he continued. 'I read an article the other day saying that our brains are probably evolving to be better at dealing with numbers because they are becoming such an important part of life. You know, telephone numbers, fax numbers, car registrations, cashpoint machine numbers, that kind of thing.'

'Crikey, I wish mine would evolve extra fast,' grinned Heather. 'I'd do better at maths then! But back to the hackers, Dad. How will your new program keep them out?'

'That's top secret!' Ray winked.

'You mean I wouldn't understand,' laughed Heather.

'Well, it is a bit technical,' admitted Ray. 'My

program is aimed at making personal firewalls stronger.'

'Firewalls?'

'A firewall is really just a pair of mechanisms – one blocks unwanted traffic and the other permits wanted traffic to pass through. Basically it just keeps idiots out of your computer system and lets you get on with what you're doing. What's more, the firewall can act as a tracing tool. My program will send an alert any time someone comes sniffing around, trying to crack the system. I may even install an auto-shutdown at that point as an extra defence mechanism. I'm not sure about that yet though. Might annoy the user too much. Anyway, the firewall my new program provides will include a virus detector as well. Mind you that will only help to pick up viruses coming from the Internet or email. I'm thinking I might tie in a general virus scanner too. People are still so lax about viruses and computer security . . . '

He trailed off and looked thoughtful.

'So your program will beat the hackers then?' Heather prompted him.

'Well, I certainly hope so, Heth,' he sighed. 'I'm pinning a lot on this program of mine. Talking of which, I'd better get back to work. And you'd better get your homework out of the way, young lady.'

Heather pulled a face.

Wednesday 19 February 2003

Heather awoke to the sound of her father singing in the bath. She smiled to hear him. He had finished his anti-hacking program and today he was launching it on the market. It had taken him longer than expected to perfect it, but now it was absolutely foolproof. There was no way any hacker could get round it. Heather knew it had cost a lot of money to write and test. Her father had been to the bank a lot over the last few months. Heather had heard him talking on the phone about remortgaging the house, whatever that was. And he'd been looking pretty worried at times. But life had gone on as usual and there'd been no shortage of treats for his favourite – and only – child.

Heather stretched and yawned and rolled out of bed. She put on her slippers and dressing gown and shuffled down to the kitchen to get the breakfast ready for them both. She hummed to herself. She was happy because her father was happy, but also because it was Anna Barry's birthday in a few days' time. They were going to go to the cinema and then to McDonald's to celebrate. Ray had promised her a new outfit for the occasion. She'd seen some really super stuff in the shopping centre in Bishopsford. She sat down with her cereal, picturing the various clothes in her mind and trying to decide which styles would look best on her.

She heard Ray padding across the landing from the bathroom to the office. He was going to check his email before coming down to the kitchen. Heather had just about decided on the black velvet leggings and the sparkly silver cardigan, when she heard a strangled cry from upstairs.

'Dad, what is it?' she called, all thoughts of outfits forgotten. She hurtled upstairs and found Ray gazing in horror at the computer screen.

'Look,' he croaked, barely able to speak. He pointed to the screen. 'I found this in my mail.'

Heather looked at the screen. It was some sort of announcement. She scanned it quickly.

> The age of hacking is here. You must
> be aware by now of all the trouble
> hackers cause to the computers in
> your world.

'Strange wording,' thought Heather to herself. She read on.

> But you probably aren't prepared at
> all, are you? Put off by the thought
> of boosting the firewalls in your
> computer, perhaps, but most likely
> put off by the cost. But now you
> needn't be. Our company, Domination
> Incorporated, has produced the
> ultimate software program that will
> make your computer 100% hackproof.

```
You need no longer fear the scourge
of hacking. Our program alerts you
as soon as anyone attempts to crack
your system. It also incorporates a
general virus scanner. And what's
more, it won't cost you anything at
all. Just download our program for
free from our website at . . .
```

Heather stopped reading in horror.

'Dad, they've stolen your idea!' she protested.

Ray was ashen faced. 'No, not really,' he sighed. 'There's no copyright in ideas, you see. The problem is that they've beaten me to the market with their program. But . . . providing it free to be downloaded – how on earth can they do it? They must have spent vast sums on research and programming, like I did. And everyone knows there's a fortune to be made in anti-hacking software but they're opting instead to offer it free. *And* ruining a lot of people like me in the process.'

'Ruining?' echoed Heather, her voice quavering.

'Yes, Heth,' said her father gently. 'I'm afraid so. Who's going to pay for anti-hacking software from me when they can get a free version from this Domination crew?' He spat out the name in disgust.

'But I bet your program is better,' said Heather loyally.

'I bet it is too,' said Ray ruefully. 'It *is* pretty darned good, though I say so myself!' He smiled weakly. 'But who's going to care? So long as this Domination program does the job, then it'll do as far as customers are concerned. That's it then,' he said, sinking his head into his hands, 'I'm ruined. All that work . . . and all for nothing.'

Heather hugged him, tears streaming down her face and fury boiling in her heart. How could Domination do this to him? And to her too? An icy feeling spread through her body as the impact of her father's words began to dawn on her. There presumably wouldn't be a new outfit now for Anna Barry's party, and maybe not for a while. Perhaps she'd have to give up her ballet lessons too.

'I don't understand,' she said, confused.

Ray looked up, red-eyed. 'It's serious, I'm afraid. I borrowed a lot of money to research and prepare my new software. I borrowed even more to launch it. No one is going to buy my program now, not with this free one on offer. I shan't earn a penny of any of that money back. I'll have to sell the house to pay my debts.'

'Oh Dad!' sobbed Heather. So it was more than new clothes and ballet lessons she'd be losing. She clung to him desperately wishing none of this was happening. But that was a wish that couldn't come true.

Friday 13 June 2003

Heather stared gloomily out of the window at the poky backyard. It was entirely paved over with cracked, grey slabs of concrete. A tall brick wall surrounded it. There were a few violets growing in the crevices, the only plants to be seen. Could so much have happened in just one year, she thought miserably.

She sighed and sat down at the table in their tiny kitchen. She hated this room and she hated the nasty little flat they lived in now. They'd been here almost three months but it felt like a year. No, more like ten years. In that time Ray had seemed to age and shrink before her eyes. After the release of the Domination program he had taken his business failure very badly. Every day he apologised endlessly to Heather about it.

Heather didn't blame her father. Not the tiniest little bit. It was all the fault of Domination Incorporated who'd stolen his idea. Domination had taken everything in her life that was good, apart from her dad, of course. Heather felt like she wasn't living any more, just existing. As well as moving from their lovely house, she'd also changed schools and hated the new one. She had no friends but she didn't want any. Anna Barry had written to her, but she hadn't written back. It just didn't seem worth it. Anna was just one of the shadows of Heather's previous life.

Since that awful day in February Ray had become completely obsessed with Domination. He spent a lot of time tracking down information about the company. But despite the fact that practically everyone had downloaded the free program, so making Domination a household name, there was surprisingly little information to be had. The company seemed to have come more or less out of nowhere. But then suddenly, practically overnight, it was world famous. The media was full of reports on it, only they were rather vague reports since no one knew where the company was based. It seemed to be a full-blown virtual company – one that existed only on the Internet. Well, it had a tiny registered office on one of the Cayman Islands to fulfil its legal obligations as a company but there was no equipment or staff there.

Every now and again, a Domination spokesperson would emerge briefly somewhere or other and allow himself or herself to be interviewed and photographed. Ray cut out the photos from the papers and stuck them up in his office. Heather looked at them from time to time. What struck her was that the people they portrayed were incredibly beautiful. They seemed to be almost perfect human beings: they had perfect figures, perfect faces, perfect hair and perfect clothes.

'They're almost too perfect to be true,' she

remarked to her father as she studied the photos in the *Daily Post*.

'Oh, they're true all right,' he muttered putting another spoon of sugar into his tea. 'All this proves it.' He gestured at their dismal surroundings. 'And so far, their wretched anti-hacking program is too perfect to be true, too,' he added morosely. 'I downloaded it and I've been running it on a test network. It seems to have taken everything into account, just like I'd done. In fact we were working on exactly the same lines. Oh, it's so sickening. I really can't believe they've beaten me to it and they're giving all their work away for nothing.'

Ray began muttering to himself, something he did a lot these days, so Heather wandered off to her bedroom. She kicked her school rucksack angrily. She rarely did her homework now so she was always in trouble at school. The principal had threatened to write to her father about it. If she had, well, he hadn't said anything. He probably wouldn't register the complaint anyway, as he was a wreck these days. He worked all day and most of the night too. Heather often saw the light shining under his bedroom door when she woke up in the night. Ray's bedroom, even pokier than her own, also served as his office. Luckily he had managed to hang on to his computers and some other office machinery even though everything else in the house had been auctioned off – all the furniture, their books and some of their clothes – to help pay off the debts. Heather preferred not to think about the day that had happened. She'd seen all her precious belongings disappear one by one into the hands of strangers. She shivered at the memory.

Ray was working on another new project at the moment. The *ultimate* ultimate virus scan, he called it. 'It'll detect every known virus, and even a few unknown ones too,' he'd sort of smiled to Heather one morning over breakfast. 'Hopefully, it'll pay to get us out of this hole.' He had glanced around in despair at the damp, cramped kitchen.

'Great!' Heather had responded, trying to smile brightly. 'I'd love to get out of here.'

★★★

The days and months dragged on, an endless round of misery at school and misery at home. Heather spent a lot of time just lying on her bed, listening to her radio. They couldn't afford to have a TV. She couldn't even be bothered to read these days. The rest of the year passed practically unnoticed. Heather was too depressed to care and Ray was manically working on new software ideas.

The New Year brought an improvement. Ray managed to sell his virus scan to a software company called Instinctive Software up in the city. They were very impressed with his work and offered him some new projects. So the day came when Heather and her father were able to leave the ghastly flat and move to a small, draughty cottage not too far from their original home. Heather went back to her old school and began to pick up the threads of her life again, and Ray began to relax. Money was tight as they were was still paying off some debts, but Heather began to feel a bit more like her old self. She was friends with Anna again so life was pretty good. For the time being anyway.

Sunday 4 April 2004

'Hey Dad!' Heather called from the kitchen. She'd just spotted the calendar. 'It's one of those funny days today – you know, when the numbers are all the same. Today is 04.04.04 or 4.4.4 I guess. I always want to write letters to people on days like this just so I can write the date out!'

'What?' Ray yawned, shuffling into the kitchen. His red hair was generously sprinkled with grey now after all the worries of the past year and his clothes were an awful lot tattier.

Heather repeated herself. Her father chuckled and sat down at the breakfast table. 'I can't remember the last time I wrote a proper letter to anyone. I'm an email guy these days.'

'I like letters,' said Heather. 'But about the date, you don't think it will cause computer problems do you? I mean, remember 9.9.99 – the ninth of September in 1999. That might have made computers go funny mightn't it, and it would have if your anti-millenium bug program hadn't stopped it.'

'That problem arose, or could have arisen, because of computer coding drawbacks – too many nines all at once. 04 or 4 doesn't have the same effect,' explained Ray.

'Good,' pronounced Heather, pouring another large bowlful of cereal. Now she was fourteen, she was almost as tall as her father. And she ate about three times as much!

'And if any weirdos want to use it as an excuse to do some hacking, they won't do very well. Most people have got hold of Domination's software and that will keep them out,' he sighed.

'Oh, shame,' pouted Heather.

'Why?' he smiled. 'Do you want doom and disaster?'

'Yes, so that then you could gallop onto the scene like a white knight on a charger and rescue the whole world with your program,' said Heather. 'That would show Domination a thing or two.'

'Loyal Heather,' smiled her father fondly, and ruffled her hair. 'Hey, turn the radio up,' he said suddenly as something caught his attention. Heather, who was closest, jumped up and turned the dial quickly.

'Domination Incorporated has just announced its profits for the first quarter of this year. The company reported profits of $3.6 billion, 45% up on last year. Domination's Chief puts this down to . . .'

'Oh, turn it off,' groaned Ray. 'It should have been me making all that money. We should be listening to this drivel from our luxury Beverley Hills home, sipping champagne and eating caviar.'

'Nonsense!' exclaimed Heather. 'We wouldn't have gone to Beverley Hills – would we?'

Ray shrugged. 'It doesn't really matter anyway, does it,' he smiled sadly. 'I didn't make a fortune.'

'No, but you *nearly* did, and there aren't many people who can claim to have done that,' protested Heather fiercely.

'You're a good girl, Heth,' replied her father. 'I'm sorry for what I've put us both through . . . '

'More tea?' Heather interrupted hastily to change the subject.

'Hmm? Oh, yes please,' he nodded. Heather filled his mug up and he shuffled back upstairs to work. Then Heather tidied away, got washed and dressed and headed off for a long walk. She didn't get back till nearly lunchtime. She was surprised to see her father hovering in the hallway, obviously looking out for her.

'Sorry . . . ' she began, a bit indignantly, but Ray interrupted her.

'Come on, come on, I've got something to show you!' He practically dragged her into the lounge and put on the TV.

'Look, I recorded this from the mid-morning bulletin.' He rewound a video tape a little way and pressed play on the remote control. After a few wiggles, a clear picture emerged. It showed a newscaster against a backdrop of a large picture of a satellite.

'*There was consternation today as the state-of-the-art, multi-billion dollar Pegasus telecommunications satellite, owned by Zeus Communications, veered briefly from its orbit . . . *' began the newscaster, but Ray butted in.

'The satellite went off course fractionally. Zeus Communications blame it on the Domination anti-hacking software it recently installed. They reckon it detected a virus or a hacker trying to break in and resisting it caused the problem. Of course, Domination are denying it but it makes you wonder. There are other reports of the same thing, look.'

Ray paused as pictures of five different satellites flashed up briefly.

'The same thing happened to those satellites, but they've all gone back on course again. And guess what? They all installed Domination's software at about the same time. Zeus are particularly annoyed because they really thought they were about to lose their satellite, and it was only launched a month ago. It cost them billions. I can't understand why the Domination program would have made that happen though.' Ray frowned.

'So does it mean the Domination stuff doesn't work properly?' asked Heather.

'Domination wouldn't admit to anything, but that's what the evidence seems to point to. And there's more.'

He fast-forwarded the video for a few seconds, then brought it back to normal speed as the backdrop on the news showed a stock exchange.

'Millions of pounds were temporarily wiped off the London stock exchange in a momentary computer glitch today. However, within seconds the problem corrected itself,

but not before widespread panic had caught hold. Over to our financial reporter . . .'

Again Ray butted in. 'And guess whose anti-hacking software the exchange was using?'

'Domination's!' guessed Heather, correctly. 'Boy, they're going to be in trouble.'

'Well, again things righted themselves and Domination deny the fault is theirs. I'm not so sure. In fact I'm beginning to wonder if maybe their software is a Trojan horse.'

'I know what the Trojan horse was,' piped up Heather. 'The Greeks used it to get themselves taken inside the enemy's camp at Troy. But I can't think what it means for computers, though.'

'More or less the same thing, Heth,' began her father. 'It's a piece of software that appears to do one thing, while in fact it carries another program, or payload, with it, usually something nasty. My suspicion is that this software of Domination is carrying a hidden logic bomb. A logic bomb is a vicious bundle of tricks. It stays quiet until a certain event triggers it off – such as today's date.' He saw Heather's startled look.

'04.04.04?' whispered Heather. 'Crikey!'

'*Just* like 04.04.04. The program explodes into action and releases a virus. Actually, "explodes" is really the wrong word. These programs usually go to work very unobtrusively to start with. Quite often they tend to spread when the computer isn't actually being used. That's done to make them harder to spot.'

'That's evil,' observed Heather.

'Yes, all viruses are,' sighed her father. 'There's no justification for them at all, like hacking. Just pure nastiness. I think I'll go and have another look through their program. I wonder if there's a back door.'

'And what's that?' asked Heather.

'Just what it sounds like really,' he explained. 'A way of accessing the program without going through the front door – the user interface that we normally see. That of course is firmly bolted to people who want to see what's going on inside it, namely hackers. I'm one of the bad guys now! But there might just be another way in. I need to get inside to see if I can find where this virus is hiding.'

'But why would Domination have set the logic bomb to go off today?' asked Heather.

'That's puzzling me too,' admitted Ray. 'But there doesn't have to be a reason. A few years back there was a horrid virus called M/97Thus which was set to destroy an infected computer's hard drive on 13 December. Just a date that appealed to the person that created the virus. Maybe his mother's birthday or his wedding anniversary or something. Who knows?'

'And even though Domination's program is meant to protect against viruses as well as hackers, it can still carry a virus?'

'Yes, the program can be trained not to act on that

particular virus. But is the virus there and, if so, where is it hiding?'

Ray disappeared upstairs. Heather turned off the video and padded to the kitchen to find something for lunch. Ray had obviously been so preoccupied with the news that he'd forgotten to get anything ready. Heather decided to do omelettes for them. She set the table for the two of them and was just cracking some eggs into a bowl, when she heard a shout from upstairs. Forgetting the eggs, she galloped upstairs at once.

'I've found it, Heth!' her father called as he heard her coming. 'I've found the hiding place!'

'Where, Dad?' panted Heather, joining him at his computer.

'Well,' he said. 'There's only a limited number of places a virus can hide. I tried looking through the command files in the operating system. That's the usual place you find them. Nothing unusual there, so I tried the cookies next. The cookies are just little bits of information about you and your computer which are left by web sites. There's always a lot of activity among the cookies, what with surfing the Net. So it's hard to find things there. But I've come across an interesting little package here that's pretending to be a cookie, but isn't. Here's our logic bomb. Now, I wonder if I can find out what it's trying to do.'

With that, he turned back to the screen. Heather

went back downstairs knowing she wouldn't be seeing him again until he'd got to the bottom of the problem, whether it took him five minutes, five hours or five weeks. She knew that look on his face. So she wasn't that surprised when she went to say goodnight to him at ten o'clock to find the omelette she'd made him for lunch and the shepherd's pie she'd brought up at teatime untouched.

'Night love,' he said absently as she kissed his cheek. He was miles away.

Heather lay awake for a while. Maybe her father could find the problem and reveal the dreadful truth about the Domination software. Then perhaps they'd be mega rich. Heather idly began to imagine all the wonderful things she could do if they had loads of money. She drifted off to sleep but woke a few hours later. She heard a thudding noise as she came to — it was Ray pacing up and down in the office.

She pulled on her dressing gown and hurried across the hall.

'Dad?' She pushed the door open hesitantly. 'Are you OK?'

Ray jumped at the sound of her voice.

'Hey? Oh, hi, love. Sorry, did I wake you?'

'Well, you are stomping around a bit,' Heather pointed out.

'Sorry!' he shrugged. 'I was thinking. You know our little logic bomb?'

Heather nodded.

'Well, I've been running the Domination program on one of my computer networks. Look what's happened.'

Heather looked at the network of two computers he pointed to. Columns and columns of gibberish were racing across the screens.

'What's that?' she gasped.

'It took me a while to figure out. At first I thought the software had just destroyed the computers' systems. But then I noticed they seemed to be working together. I think they've been taken over!'

Heather shook her head, not understanding, and perched on a stack of boxes of paper.

'You know the SETI@home project, don't you? It's connected with the Arecibo Radio Telescope in Puerto Rico and has been going since 1999.'

Heather frowned in puzzlement. Then her face cleared. 'Oh, you mean the Search for Extra-Terrestrial Intelligence? People all over the world donate a bit of their computer's power to the project.'

'Spot on!' smiled her dad. 'When their computers are idle, the software downloads a chunk of SETI data and analyses it. It uses thousands, maybe millions, of Internet-connected PCs. Well, this what seems to be going on here. Domination are trying to get the world's computer systems to work together. It'll cripple *everything* that relies on computers – it'll be a billion times worse than the millennium bug was meant to be. Just think of what computers do these days. They command traffic systems, weapons systems, financial transactions, life-saving machines in hospitals, production processes in factories! They store vast quantites of highly sensitive data. They're everywhere! If they stop working properly, so does the world. My guess is that this logic bomb of theirs is substituting their own security files so that they can hijack computing time whenever they want. No one would know where an attack on a computer system is coming from. They could hack into bank accounts and make it look like it's my computer that did it! They could launch a nuclear missile at Russia and make everyone believe that the command came from a computer in the Pentagon. And imagine, this bomb of theirs is infecting every computer system and network as we speak. It'll be all over the World Wide Web by now. It's everywhere!' Ray smashed his fist against the bookcase and sent a handful of computer manuals crashing to the floor.

'But why?' faltered Heather. 'It just doesn't make sense, unless it's meant to be some kind of a joke. Pretty sick joke, though.'

'It's more serious than a joke, Heth.' He stopped pacing around for a moment. 'It's disastrous. It's catastrophic.'

'What can we do?' cried Heather, jumping up. 'We've got to warn people!'

'Yes, but I need to do a bit more work first. I need

to find out a bit more about the virus they have embedded in the program. It may be irreversible. And if it is, then the world's in an awful lot of trouble.'

Ray sat down in front of his computer and began rattling away at the keyboard. Heather watched him for a while as he typed in strings of incomprehensible commands at lightning speed. Her mind was in turmoil. Just when everything looked like being OK again, here was more trouble – deadly serious trouble.

Monday 5 April 2004

Heather woke early, despite the fact she'd hardly slept since her talk with her father during the night. Her head felt heavy. She heard the front door bang. Ray was never normally up at this hour – he must have been up all night! She dragged herself out of bed and shuffled in her slippers to the kitchen. Ray had left her a note that read: *Gone to get the papers*! For a moment Heather couldn't understand why because he didn't normally bother with papers. Then she realised. He'd want to read up about all the various computer glitches of the day before and see if anyone else shared his suspicions of what Domination's software was up to.

Ray was soon back with an armful of papers. He threw them onto the kitchen table with a groan.

'There must be at least half a tree's worth of paper there,' he grumbled. 'And look at my hands. Black as ink, literally!' He turned his hands palms up to show Heather. 'You don't get this with nice clean new technology like computers!'

'True, but you don't get all the show-biz gossip and cartoons,' Heather pointed out, pulling a few of the tabloids out from the pile. 'I'll read these ones for you, if you like.'

'Don't be late for school,' warned Ray.

'It's OK,' explained Heather, 'I've got an hour

before I have to get the bus. What am I looking for, exactly? Any mention of Domination?'

'Any mention of *anything* to do with computer problems yesterday,' he replied. 'And yes, of course, anything about that wretched company.'

They sat down at the table and began to leaf through the papers. Heather kept getting distracted by interesting looking articles and photos. It was hard to ignore them.

'Found anything yet?' asked Ray, a few moments later. 'There's something in the *Daily Times* about the satellites but it reports that it was just a temporary aberration that "confirms that the company believes it has nothing to do with Domination software". They must be joking!'

Heather guiltily flicked to the business pages of the tabloid paper she was reading – well, business half page. She'd been deep into an article about her favourite pop group when he'd spoken.

'Um, um, oh yes, here we are!' Her eye fell on a mention of Domination. *Software hitch hits satellites* was the heading of the short paragraph. 'Here, Dad, listen to this. "All of the satellites owned by telecommunications giant, Zeus, threatened to hurtle off into space yesterday. The space machinery began to creak as a suspected hacker or virus prepared to invade. However, within seconds, Domination's combined anti-virus and anti-hacking software apparently cut in and oiled the works. Says

Domination Chief Henrik Sanderson, 'This is exactly what we expected. The fact that things returned to normal within a fraction of a second proves that our software worked. You are guaranteed protection from any hacker or virus-related problem with our software.' " I wonder where they managed to dig Henrik out from? Domination are usually hard to pin down, aren't they?'

There was a photo of a smiling Henrik Sanderson. Heather hated to admit it, but the guy was amazingly good looking. Perfect, like all the Domination people she'd seen in the media.

Ray flicked through some more papers. 'They all say the same thing,' he groaned. 'Everyone's perfectly happy that the software is working correctly. Nobody's querying it at all, not even the stock exchange. Honestly, the exchange threatened to crash completely and bankrupt Britain and no one raises an eyebrow. It's ridiculous!'

'Why don't you write to the papers?' suggested Heather. 'Tell them what you suspect.'

'Good idea! I will, but I doubt they'll be interested,' he sighed. 'I'll write to everyone I can think of. I'll telephone and email too. I just need to do a bit more work on how the virus is acting to see if it's reversible. I can prove that it's there in the cookies but the hard part will be to get people to listen. People don't like to be told they've been made fools of!'

'Go for it, Dad!' said Heather encouragingly, pushing the papers away and getting up from the table. Time to get dressed and head for the bus.

Monday 26 April 2004

'Why will no one listen to me?' Ray sank his head in his hands.

For the umpteenth time, he'd just been told politely but firmly by a senior manager of a company he'd phoned that they were quite satisfied with the Domination software they were using. As usual, they'd thanked him for his concern over any possible problems that might lie ahead. However, they didn't feel the need to discuss it further.

Ray had finished his work on the virus in the Domination program. He'd discovered that it was reversible, but the longer it remained in a computer system, the more damage it did and the more difficult it became to correct. He'd managed to adapt his anti-virus program to tackle the Domination virus. For the last three weeks, Ray had been writing to various influential people and companies about his fears but he'd had no response at all. He'd written to papers and to TV and radio stations. He'd sent emails to all the corners of the earth and posted notices in loads of forums on the Web but no one had paid any attention.

'Time's running out, Heth!' he groaned. 'What do we do?'

Heather shrugged. 'I just don't know, Dad! You've tried everything. We'd better just prepare ourselves for the worst. Remember before the millennium when some people went crazy and stocked up with tinned food and batteries and medical supplies and stuff? Maybe we'd better do that sort of thing. Mind you, we don't know what Domination are planning to do once they've crippled all the world's computers.'

'Nothing very nice I expect,' said her father grimly. 'We're looking at a breakdown of civilisation here. This time round it could really be TEOWAWKI – The End Of the World As We Know It.'

'Surely it won't be that bad, will it, Dad?' Heather asked anxiously. She found it impossible to believe that doomsday was just around the corner.

'It will, love, it will!' he began pacing the room, his face a mask of consternation. 'That virus of theirs is totally destructive. With computer systems gone, the world is helpless. We might have to think about moving into the country. All cities and towns will be nightmare areas when all public services stop functioning. You know, thousands of people in America left their homes in the mid 1990s to set up self-sufficient communities because they were worried about what would happen when the millennium dawned. It's still not too late for us to do something like that.'

Heather couldn't quite picture herself and her dad milking cows and grinding corn but she didn't say anything.

Suddenly the doorbell rang. It made them both jump.

'I'll get it,' announced Heather, grateful to be dragged away from her imaginings of the horrendous effects of the Domination virus.

A smart, petite woman stood on the doorstep.

'Hello, I'm Susan McCarthy,' she smiled brightly and held out a hand to Heather. Heather took it warily. Susan had a firm, cool handshake. 'You must be Heather.'

'Yes,' admitted Heather, suspiciously.

'I hoped I might be able to see your father. I'm with the *Daily Post*. Your father wrote to us a few weeks back. I only came across his letter today. I'm very interested in what he has to say. May I talk with him?'

'Yes, of course!' Heather practically pulled Susan over the doorstep. At last here was someone who was listening.

'Dad!' she yelled. 'Here's a journalist to see you!'

'Thank heavens!' exclaimed Ray, sticking his head out of the office. He didn't give Susan a chance to introduce herself. 'Come here and I'll show you just what I'm talking about,' he beckoned enthusiastically.

Heather hurried Susan to the office. Ray was already seated at the computer, calling up his data on the Domination software.

'Hello, I'm Susan . . .' Susan began her introduction again.

'Delighted to meet you, Susan. I'm Ray, as you know,' he smiled, shooting a sidelong glance at the journalist as he called up the Domination program on his computer. 'Now, this is what I'm talking about.' And Ray launched into a detailed explanation of his findings. Susan scribbled away furiously. Heather smiled as she left them to it. This Susan looked efficient. With any luck she'd get her father's story into the papers.

Two hours later, Susan and Ray were still in conference. Heather decided she'd better offer them tea and biscuits. She went into the office and found Susan peering at the computer over Ray's shoulder. Her shorthand notebook lay discarded on her chair. The look on her face showed that she was convinced by what Ray was telling her.

'Sorry to interrupt,' Heather said, 'but do you want something to eat?'

Susan and Ray turned to her, both wearing that slightly puzzled expression that people have when they've been totally engrossed in something and are now being reluctantly dragged away from it.

'It's teatime,' explained Heather patiently. 'I thought you might be hungry.'

Susan glanced at her watch.

'Gracious, so it is! I'd love a cuppa, and I need a comfort break too. Where's the bathroom, please?'

'Next door,' said Heather, hoping it wasn't too untidy. She and her father weren't used to guests and the bathroom was the general dumping ground for dirty washing, wellington boots and magazines.

'Back in a tick,' said Susan and disappeared.

'Well?' whispered Heather. 'Does she believe you?'

'She certainly does! She's pretty clued up on computer matters. She's a freelance reporter, but she's sure her editor will want this story. She's very excited about it.'

'Excited!' echoed Heather in disgust. 'She ought to be *terrified*!'

'Journalists are never terrified,' smiled her father. 'The more scary, the more they like something!'

'Absolutely right!' laughed Susan, coming back into the room. She was pulling a comb through her long, dark hair. 'And your Dad's story is *very* scary.'

'It's not a story,' protested Heather. 'It's the truth!'

'And I believe it,' said Susan, emphatically. 'Now, Ray, a few more things I need to know.' The two of them were back at the computer so Heather trudged down to the kitchen to put the kettle on. She felt annoyed, but she wasn't exactly sure why. She ought to be pleased that at last someone was prepared to champion her dad's cause.

'I'm just jealous, I guess,' she muttered to herself as she filled the kettle at the sink. 'I like having Dad to myself. Oh!'

The exclamation came as a shadow flitted across the window in front of her. She stepped back, heart thumping. Whatever was it? She peered out again into the garden nervously, but there was nothing to be seen in the evening gloom. She put the kettle down, and went to the back door. She quietly opened it and listened. Nothing. Nothing at all.

'Must have been a cat or a bird or something,' she shrugged, returning to her tea-making duties. 'I'm just cracking up!' But she felt slightly uneasy all the same. She quickly brewed up and grabbed some biscuits and headed back to the office.

It was another hour before Susan left. She looked very pleased with herself as she and Ray came out of the office at last.

'I shall go straight to the office and type this up now,' she announced.

'I thought you journalists all had laptops and modems and didn't need to go to the office any more,' said Heather.

Susan pulled a face. 'Tell my editor that! Mind you, a lot of us prefer the old-fashioned methods. Gives you a bit of thinking time before putting an article together. So, front page tomorrow, I guarantee! This is a sensation. I'll talk to you tomorrow, Ray.'

This time Ray shook hands with Susan and beamed at her. He was still beaming as he and Heather watched Susan drive off.

'Wow, front page news!' exclaimed Heather. 'Dad, you're going to be famous!'

'Yes, it looks like I am!' he agreed happily.

This time Heather was up as early as her father to nip down to the paper shop.

'I can't wait!' said Heather, so excited that she bounced around in her seat in the car. 'You'll really get people talking. You'll save the world yet, Dad!'

'I hope so,' he smiled, feeling rather pleased with himself.

He pulled up right opposite the paper shop. Normally Ray was a very considerate road user, always parking off the main road. But today he was in too much of a hurry. Heather was almost out of the car before it had stopped moving. She ran round the back of it, and clucked in exasperation as a string of cars appeared from nowhere and delayed them crossing the road. She grabbed her father's hand and they jogged across and into the shop.

'The *Daily Post*, where is it?' she muttered, scanning the shelves. Then she spotted a pile of folded papers. She seized one and shook it open. Ray looked over her shoulder eagerly. But then they turned to each other and said in unison: 'It's not there!'

For a second they gazed at each other in disappointment, then Heather pulled herself together.

'Maybe it's on an inside page – perhaps the front page was already sorted out by the time Susan got to the office.'

'Maybe,' said Ray, but not very hopefully. If Susan had said the revelation about Domination was worthy of the front page, then he believed her. He watched anxiously as Heather leafed through the paper. But every page was full of other news. No mention of the infected Domination anti-hacking software anywhere.

'Oh, Dad, what a shame!' Heather felt like crying. She'd been so sure her father was about to get the recognition he deserved. She wouldn't have minded a bit of the reflected glory either! She folded the paper up awkwardly. It looked very tatty after its rough handling.

'Come on, let's pay for it and go home,' said Ray despondently. 'I'll give Susan a ring when we get back. She gave me her home and office numbers. I'd like to find out what happened with her story.'

But Susan wasn't at home. He left a message on her answer-phone. Then he tried the *Daily Post* offices. Heather lurked behind him and strained her ears to listen in on the conversation.

'May I speak to Susan McCarthy, please?' asked Ray politely when the receptionist answered.

'Susan? One moment, please.' Some cheerful tinned music floated out from the phone. Suddenly it stopped.

'I'm sorry, we think Susan must be ill. She was due at the office last night but didn't arrive. Have you tried her home number?' asked the receptionist.

'What?' cried Ray. 'But when she left me yesterday evening, she said she was going straight to the office. She had a story to write up.'

'Oh. Can you hold, please caller. I'll try and find Susan's editor.' The music resumed.

'Dad, what's happened?' asked Heather in alarm. 'Did she say Susan didn't arrive last night?'

'Yes, I just can't believe it,' he replied, running his fingers through his hair distractedly. 'She told me she was going straight there. I wonder what happened?'

'Perhaps she broke down or something,' suggested Heather. 'Or maybe she was taken ill.'

'Did she look ill to you when she left here?' demanded her father

'Well, no, but—'

'Hang on, the receptionist's back.' Ray heard the music stop.

'May I take your name please, caller?' enquired the receptionist.

'Ray Mayhew,' he replied automatically. 'But, look here, does the editor know anything about Susan?'

'And your phone number, please?'

'Never mind that, now,' Ray interrupted. 'I'd like to speak to the editor immediately. Susan had an extremely important story for him.'

'The editor is in a meeting at the moment, but he'll get back to you as soon as possible if you'll give me your number,' said the receptionist curtly.

Ray had to admit defeat. He wearily reeled off the

phone number and put the phone down.

'What sort of a paper is it?' he complained to Heather. 'They seem to have lost a reporter with the news scoop of the year and they don't seem to care. I don't suppose the editor will bother to phone,' he sighed. 'I'll just have to try again later and see if Susan has turned up.'

Heather got ready for school, annoyed at her father not being in the paper. She was still pretty peeved as she walked back along the lane to the cottage that evening. A bad day at school hadn't helped – bad because her audition for the school play had been awful. Heather had hoped to get one of the main roles but now she reckoned she'd be lucky if she even got a walk-on part.

'Oh well,' she muttered angrily to herself, 'who wants to be in a rotten old play anyway.'

She kicked a stone along the road and then turned into her gateway. Then she gasped. Parked outside the front door of the cottage was a police car.

'Dad!' she shrieked, rushing up the path. Something dreadful must have happened to him. She burst through the front door.

'What's happened? Dad?' she yelled.

'Here, love,' came Ray's voice from the tiny sitting room. Heather hurtled in. Her father was sitting by the window, looking pale and nervous, but otherwise OK. Opposite him sat two policemen, one with a notebook out.

'What's going on, Dad?' asked Heather in a slightly shaky voice.

But one of the police officers answered.

'Good afternoon, Miss Mayhew,' he said. 'We're here making enquiries following the disappearance of Susan McCarthy.'

'Disappearance?' gasped Heather.

'I'm afraid so, Heth,' said Ray gently. 'Apparently, no one has seen or heard from Susan since she left here last night.'

'Her car was found about two miles from here a few hours ago,' added the police officer. 'It had been concealed in a wood. But there's no sign of Miss McCarthy. As you and your father were the last people to see her, we're here to ask you some questions.'

'What sort of questions?' Heather's mind was racing. Did they think she and her father had murdered Susan and buried her in the garden or something?

'We just want to find out anything we can that might be useful, Miss Mayhew,' said the other officer. 'Your father has told us about his meeting with Miss McCarthy, what time she left and where she was going. Now, is there anything *you* can tell us?'

Heather shook her head, bewildered. What was there to tell?

'Did you notice anything unusual last night? Did you see anyone hanging around? Perhaps you—'

But Heather had stopped listening. The shadow!

She'd just remembered that strange shadow that had flitted past the window. But surely that was nothing. After all, she'd had a look around and not seen anything. However, it was worth mentioning.

'I *might* have seen something,' she ventured.

'Yes?' asked the police officer encouragingly.

'Did you?' said Ray, astonished.

'I saw a shadow,' Heather said. It sounded foolish to her ears. 'I was making a cup of tea for Dad and Susan – Miss McCarthy – and I went to fill the kettle when I thought I saw a sort of shadowy shape go by the window.'

'You *thought* you saw?' queried the first police officer.

'Yes, well, no, I mean, I really don't know if it was anything or not.' Heather was flustered.

'Take your time, love,' Ray soothed her. 'Tell us what you think you saw.'

Heather took a deep breath. She recreated the scene in her mind's eye.

'As I was saying, I was at the sink when a shadow, well, more a shadowy movement, made me jump. I thought maybe it was a bird or a cat. I opened the door and looked outside but there wasn't anything there. That's it.'

The second officer was scribbling furiously in his notebook.

'How big was this shadow?' he asked.

'I don't know,' replied Heather. 'I was just aware of

a sudden flicker of shadow. I can't tell you how big or what it was or anything I'm afraid. Something made me jump and that's all I can say really. At the time I thought it must be a bird flying close to the window or a cat jumping down from the roof.'

She felt very unhelpful.

'Will you show me where you were standing when this happened?' asked the second officer.

'Yes, of course, if you think it helps,' said Heather. She was surprised they were taking what she said so seriously.

She led the officer to the kitchen. He peered out of the window and then went outside to poke around for a while. Heather went back to the sitting room. The other policeman was running through what Ray had told them again. Heather only half listened. She was suddenly very frightened at the thought that someone might have been lurking outside the house last night. Someone who then went on to kidnap poor Susan – or even worse. Suddenly her blood ran cold. A terrible thought crossed her mind. What if it was someone from Domination who had somehow learned that Susan was about to expose them and their destructive software? But how would they have done that? How would they have known Susan was coming here? And how would they have known where she and her father lived anyway? That last question was easily answered, Heather realised with a feeling of dread.

Ray had been writing and emailing letters of warning. Perhaps Domination had intercepted one of those messages, or someone had told them about his warning. That was entirely possible.

But why had Susan been kidnapped and not her or her dad? That's what she couldn't understand. Unless, of course, it was pure coincidence that the kidnapper had turned up while Susan was here. Presumably he'd worked out who or what Susan was and saw that she was a more immediate danger than Ray. Maybe he'd decided to get rid of Susan first and then come back for her and Dad. Oh no! Heather suddenly felt faint.

'What's up?' she heard Ray's worried voice. It seemed to come from a long distance away. She felt dizzy and wobbly. Blindly she fumbled for the nearest chair and sank into it. She groaned and leaned forward to put her head between her knees.

'She's fainted!' Ray's distant voice sounded again. She felt his arm around her but she couldn't acknowledge it. It was taking all her concentration at the moment not to be sick. Sweat was pouring off her even though she felt freezing cold. It was a ghastly feeling. Eventually the nausea ebbed away and she gingerly lifted her head from her knees. Bright lights swam before her eyes so she quickly plonked her head back down again.

'Feeling better?' asked Ray.

'A bit,' Heather admitted.

'Shall I fetch some water?' asked the policeman.

Heather shook her head feebly.

'No thanks,' interpreted her father.

Just then the other officer returned.

'Did you find anything?' Ray asked.

'No. No footprints or signs of damage to the plants out there. As your daughter says, it probably was a bird or an animal. But it was worth checking out. Is she OK?' He'd just noticed Heather's strange position.

'No, she fainted. It's all been a horrible shock,' replied Ray. 'Now, if you've finished your questions, I'd like to get her to bed for a lie-down please.'

'Of course, sir,' said the policeman. 'Thank you for your cooperation. We'll keep you informed of our progress. We'll see our own way out.'

Heather heard their footsteps receding down the hall and then the thump of the front door slamming behind them. She lifted her head again. No bright lights this time. She looked up at Ray. She could see at once that he was worried.

'It was Domination, wasn't it?' she croaked. 'They got Susan.'

'Yes. It was Domination,' he said firmly. 'We're getting out of here just as soon as I've packed a few things.'

'But won't that make the police think we're guilty of something?' Heather asked anxiously.

'Frankly I'd rather have them think that than hang around here for a visit from Domination. They're probably watching us right now!' replied her father grimly.

'Oh no! How will we get away?' whimpered Heather.

'We'll just have to pretend we're going swimming and act as naturally as we can. Now, just pack a few necessities into your sports bag for both of us – you know, change of clothes, towel, toothbrush – and I'll stow my laptop and all my evidence about Domination into another bag. I just need to disable my desktop computers so they won't be able to find anything there. It won't take long.'

'Don't forget money and cheque books and stuff,' Heather, practical as ever, reminded him.

'What? Oh, good girl, of course. Better take passports too, I guess. Leave that to me.'

Heather hurried off to her room, her heart pounding. What if Domination arrived on the doorstep before they were packed? And anyway, what on earth *do* you pack when you're fleeing from home, possibly running for your life? Heather felt shaky again. This was really scary. What about food? Should she pack some? And what about things like the library books that were due back, and the electricity bill and the telephone bill and . . .

'Stop it!' she told herself, angrily. Right now, those things just weren't important. All that mattered was getting away safely before she and her dad disappeared like poor Susan. With any luck, they'd be able to expose Domination to, well, to someone important, and the whole thing would be over in days. She rifled through her chest of drawers and stuffed some clean underwear and a couple of T-shirts into the bag. She came across two baseball hats. They might be useful for disguise purposes, so she packed those too, and a pair of sunglasses, even though it was a cloudy spring day. She quickly changed into her comfiest tracksuit and trainers and then dug around in the clean washing pile for some clothes for her dad. Next, she grabbed some toiletries from the bathroom.

'I'm nearly ready!' Ray called.

Heather nipped back into her room. She quickly hid her jewellery box down the bed, just in case Domination or anyone else had a poke round her room, but not before she took out the silver locket she'd been given as a christening present and her mother's wedding ring. She zipped those into an inside pocket. She took a last look round the room and her eye fell on Buster, her old, very tatty toy dog. She couldn't leave Buster behind! Into the bag he went. There was just enough space.

'Right, I'm through,' said Ray, appearing at the bedroom doorway. He held a bulging sports bag. No one would guess it wasn't full of sports gear.

'Now, nice and casual out of the house,' he said. 'We're just off for a swim, remember.'

Heather swallowed hard. She felt terrified but she

tried not to let it show. As calmly as she could, she stepped out through the front door.

'Got all your swimming stuff, love?' asked Ray, a little louder than usual as he turned and locked the door behind them.

'Yep, I think so!' Heather forced a smile.

'OK, off we go then,' said her father.

They climbed into the car and set off. Heather allowed herself a surreptitious look back. Maybe she was just imagining it, but the bush near the gate seemed to be swaying a lot – and there was no wind today.

'I think there was someone in the garden, Dad,' she said shakily.

'Very probably,' he replied grimly. 'Hang in there, love, we've got away.'

'For now,' Heather added under her breath.

They drove for about fifty miles, and then Ray turned down a quiet country lane and stopped the car.

'Where are we, Dad?' asked Heather.

'I'm not entirely sure,' he grinned. 'But this place is perfect. I have a little job to do.'

He climbed out of the car and walked round and opened the boot. He rummaged around for something.

'Aha! Here they are!' he said.

'Here what are?' demanded Heather.

She got out and went round to join him. He was

holding a small screwdriver and a set of number plates, which didn't match the car's. She looked at Ray, puzzled. He crouched down and began to unscrew the proper plates off the car.

'Years back, before you were born, Mum and I had a little green car. Well, we got caught in a concertina crash in it – that's when a line of cars bump into each other. It wasn't serious, but both the front and back number plates got broken. So I went out the next day to get a new set of plates for the car, and so did your mum! So we ended up with two sets. I hung onto the spare set, even after we sold the car – you know how I hate to throw things away! I've kept them in the boot all this time. It's totally illegal, I'm well aware, but we'll have to use them. It may buy us a few extra days. I shall confess to the police once this business is all over.' He sighed as he removed the proper number plate, and replaced it with the false one.

Heather watched him silently and followed him to the front of the car as he repeated the process there. Things were getting really serious for her father to do something like this. He normally respected the law.

They drove off again. Soon they came to a small town. Ray found a branch of his bank and withdrew a lot of money. Heather watched wide-eyed as the notes plopped out.

'Crikey, why are you getting so much money out?'

she asked. 'Isn't it risky? I mean, we might get mugged.'

'Don't worry, we'll be running too fast from Domination for any other crooks to get us,' smiled her father. 'We need to use cash while we're on the run,' he explained. 'Credit cards can be traced, you see. And knowing Domination, once they realise we've flown the coop, which I imagine they will do in about an hour or so, they'll start using every means within their power to track us down.'

'Uh-oh,' Heather pulled a face.

'Hey, don't worry, love,' said Ray, giving her a hug. 'Your old dad is a match for them. We'll avoid leaving any electronic trails behind us so they'll have nothing to go on. Now, let's hit the road again. I want to get a fair bit further tonight.'

They set off again, but, as Heather soon realised, back in the direction they'd come from. She pointed this out to her father.

'That's right,' he explained. 'Our cash withdrawal is traceable. If either the police or Domination plot the route we took from home, they'll logically assume that we kept on going in a straight line from home and will concentrate searches for us in the west. So by turning back east, we buy ourselves some extra time.'

'Good thinking, Dad!' said Heather, admiringly. Her father was more worldly-wise than he'd ever made out.

A few hours, and two hundred miles later, he pulled in at a motorway service station and travel lodge.

'We'll stay here tonight,' he told Heather. 'We'll get a room, and then I need you to do some shopping for me. These motorway places usually have a good selection of stuff. I shall need a razor, shaving cream and, if possible, some hair dye. I'm afraid we may need to change your hair colour too.'

'Wow, this is real cloak and dagger stuff,' grinned Heather. She was beginning to feel a bit happier now they were so far from home. 'I think I'll go for red hair. Louise Smith dyed her hair red last month. Her mum went nuts, she said, but she looked really cool.'

'And I'm sure you will too,' smiled her father. 'Somehow I don't think the same will apply to me without my beard, though! That'll be a real shock to the system. I haven't shaved for about twenty years!'

Heather giggled.

There were plenty of spare rooms at the travel lodge. The receptionist hardly glanced at them when they booked in as Mr John O'Neill and his daughter Emma. Ray paid for the room there and then. Next he unpacked and Heather trotted off to do the shopping. The shop only had a few shades of hair dye available, but one of these was a nice mahogany shade which was near enough to red. Heather chose a rich brown for Ray, smiling to herself at the thought of what they'd both look like in an hour's time. She got the razor too! Heather was starting to enjoy the adventure. It was better than your average Tuesday.

'So let's make plans,' said Ray, half an hour later as he and Heather sat on the bed with plastic caps over their wet, dyed hair. His cheeks and chin were now smooth and shiny, except for the odd, red sore patch where he had cut himself shaving. There had been a lot of swearing during the procedure. Now he looked completely different. Heather kept stealing glances at him, trying to get used to this new dad.

'We probably don't have long,' he pointed out.

'But surely, now we're disguised . . . ' began Heather.

'That'll help, but we need to be realistic. If, or rather, when the police come looking for me again in connection with Susan's disappearance, and find the house empty, they'll jump to the wrong conclusion and think I'm the guilty party. There'll be a full-scale search and they'll soon track us down, even with dyed hair and false number plates on the car.'

'But we've given Domination the slip, haven't we?' said Heather.

'Again, only for the moment. With their technology, they're probably even now trying to trace us. They'll be hacking into the computer systems of hotels and motorway stations to try to find us. They'll have engineered the firewalls in their so-called anti-hacking software to permit *them* to get through, no question. You saw how the receptionist entered our details on her computer, didn't you? Well, Domination will probably try to find our credit card number first, and when that doesn't work, I expect they'll hunt for any father/daughter bookings. The false name won't deter them. Let's just hope there are a lot of fathers and daughters travelling around at the moment. That'll give them more leads to follow.'

Ray was quiet for a moment. Things weren't looking too hopeful.

'So, what do we do?' asked Heather.

'I always think better over food,' he replied. 'Besides, I think it's time to wash this stuff out of our hair anyway. We'll finish off here, then go and find some supper and make our plans.'

Ray was first to complete his transformation. Heather gasped as he stepped out of the bathroom, towelling his dark brown hair dry.

'Cool, Dad!' she smiled. 'Even *I* don't recognise you!'

Ray admired himself in the mirror. 'Yes, not bad at all.'

'My turn!' Heather hurried into the bathroom and washed the hair dye out over the sink. Then she cautiously looked at her reflection. Wow! It really suited her. She looked better even than Louise Smith. Wait till her friends saw her! If, that is, they ever did . . .

She shook her head crossly. Mustn't think like that.

'Here Dad,' she called. 'How do I look then?'

'About five years older, young lady. Very nice, actually, although I'm sure I'm not meant to say that. It's a bad sign when parents approve of what their children do, isn't it?'

'Nonsense,' laughed Heather. 'You're so sweet, you'd approve of anything I did. Just so long as I look different, that's all that matters.'

A quick blast with the hairdryer and then they were ready to go for tea. Ray packed up his laptop and the precious CDs that stored all his programs into his sports bag.

'These are going *everywhere* with me from now on,' he promised.

The café was quiet so Ray and Heather found a corner table. Over their sausage and chips they plotted what they would do the next day.

'I've got to get publicity out about Domination, and fast,' said Ray, glancing over his shoulder just in case anyone was lurking. 'What's the best way to do that, do you think?'

'Could you go to a TV station, or radio station and demand to go on air?' suggested Heather, chasing some beans round her plate with her fork.

'That's an idea,' he nodded. 'But I bet there's a constant stream of lunatics all trying to voice their opinions that way already. I'd just be one more. I expect they have very good systems in place for stopping people barging into studios.'

'Yes, I expect you're right,' sighed Heather. 'So how else could you get publicity?'

'There's the newspapers, parliament and industry,' Ray reeled off the remaining possibilities.

'Industry? How do you mean?' frowned Heather.

'Well, you'd have to pick the right industry, of course. I mean, a large company with a lot of clout, something like Zeus Communications. In fact,' Ray warmed to his theme, 'Zeus would be ideal. The company's already experienced a hiccup from Domination's software – on the 4th, remember? Although things corrected themselves there was some real concern at the time. So, with any luck, there may be a seed of doubt in their minds. We just need to nurture it. If I can only get the managing director to look at my programs, he'll see at once there's a big, big problem. Now, what's his name? Montgomery, Lucien Montgomery, I think.'

He paused to take a few more mouthfuls of chips.

'Zeus is based up in the city, isn't it?' asked Heather. 'So we'll head up there tomorrow, then? But won't they have anti-lunatic procedures too?'

'Possibly,' mused Ray. 'But hopefully they won't be as good as TV and radio stations. And anyway, I might be able to make the managing director see me.' He smiled wickedly.

'How?' demanded Heather.

'You'll see,' he said, mysteriously. 'We'll need to pop into a supermarket tomorrow, first thing. Then I must call on the one person I think we can trust.'

'Who?' asked Heather, surprised. She couldn't think of anyone who fitted that bill at the moment.

'Marcus Reidy. He's with the software company I do all my work for these days. He hasn't been there long. I've talked to him a good few times and we get on really well. He was very sympathetic when I told him about my bad luck with the anti-hacking software. Like me, he doesn't approve of what Domination did when they gave the software away free. I'm *sure* he's trustworthy.'

'But why do we need him, Dad? I thought we could do this on our own.' Heather felt a bit aggrieved.

'He'll be our back-up, plus he adds a bit of credibility to my claims. If I can get him to endorse my program, it may help persuade the Zeus MD to take me seriously. Marcus and his company, Instinctive Software, are becoming very well known,' Ray explained.

Heather nodded. 'I've heard of it. We've got some of their software at school.'

'If I can run through my program with him and get him to make some more copies of my CDs then, if anything happens to me, he can carry on what we're doing.'

Hearing her father say 'if anything happens to me' made Heather shiver. She didn't need to ask him what he meant. She knew exactly what he meant –

if he disappeared like Susan. Heather tried not to think about the fact that she could disappear too . . .

'So, we need to make an early start. Do you want some pudding? We'd better build our strength up.' Ray stacked up their empty plates.

'You bet! I'll have chocolate fudge cake and ice cream please, plus another Coke,' said Heather, greedily.

'You got it,' said Ray, and disappeared up to the serving counter.

Heather sat and wondered about what the next day would bring. It certainly wasn't going to be dull!

Wednesday 28 April 2004

It was still dark when Ray shook Heather awake. 'Come on, we need to be off.'

Heather groaned and squinted at her watch.

'It's only 6 o'clock,' she grumbled.

'I know,' he soothed, 'but it's a two hour drive to the city, and we've got a busy day, remember?'

Heather wasn't likely to forget. The thoughts of last night flashed through her mind. She stretched and rolled out of bed. She was surprised to see that Ray had already packed their bags, just leaving out some clothes for her.

'Gosh, what time did you get up?' she yawned.

'A long while ago,' he smiled wearily. 'I had a lot of thinking to do, and I had to type up some stuff about my research on Domination's software to give to Marcus and Zeus.' He waved a handful of CDs at her. 'I think I've thought of everything.'

'I'm sure you have, Dad,' agreed Heather, pulling on her T-shirt and jumper. 'Will there be time for breakfast, I'm—'

'Starving, I know,' grinned Ray. 'Here we are, cup of tea and a few biscuits. Will that do?'

'Perfect, thanks,' said Heather, tying up her runners.

She soon finished breakfast, and they gathered up their belongings and went out to the car. Dad left the key at the empty reception desk.

Heather settled back in the passenger seat and watched the sleepy world wake up as they sped along towards the city. At first they practically had the road to themselves, but the traffic gradually started building up. Heather leant forward and fiddled with the car radio. It was just 7 o'clock, and they caught the news headlines. There'd been flooding on the west coast due to an extremely high tide. Some scandal or other had erupted concerning a politician Heather had never heard of. She was just beginning to daydream, when the next announcement made her jerk forward.

'Police are continuing to search for missing journalist Susan McCarthy, last seen in Redwood on 26 April. Police are anxious to contact Mr Ray Mayhew of Redwood, the last person to see Ms McCarthy, in order to eliminate him from their enquiries. He disappeared from his home yesterday with his fourteen-year-old daughter, Heather, shortly after police interviewed him…' The announcer went on to give a brief description of both of them, together with their car registration.

'Wrong on all counts now!' gloated Heather, quickly recovering from her initial shock at hearing themselves mentioned on the news.

'Drat!' cursed Ray. 'I didn't think they'd be onto us this quickly. As for eliminating me from their enquiries, I don't quite believe that. They almost certainly think I'm responsible for poor Susan's disappearance, which, indirectly, I am,' he sighed. 'If she hadn't got caught up in this she'd still be safe.'

'Oh no, Dad,' protested Heather. 'You can't blame yourself for that. She came to us, remember? I'm sorry she's been kidnapped, of course, but we didn't do it. Domination did.'

'I know, love,' he agreed. 'I know. I'm just feeling a bit weighed down at the moment. We should manage to stay out of the clutches of the police for a while longer. Let's hope so anyway.'

Heather began to feel very on edge. Suddenly she spotted a police car coming in the opposite direction. She froze in her seat but it sailed past. A glance at her father's face told her that he had shared her worry. He caught her eye and smiled. 'We must stop feeling so guilty!' he laughed. 'They haven't got us yet.'

They drove on, and presently came to the outskirts of the city. Ray noticed a small supermarket that was just opening.

'Few bits of shopping to get,' he said, pulling in outside. 'I'll nip in on my own.' With that he was out of the car. Heather had been just about to say she'd come too as she didn't want to be left all alone. But her father on his own would attract less attention than with her, especially after the radio alert.

Heather gazed idly out of the window. A lad of about fifteen or sixteen was leaning his bike up against a wall. He turned and saw Heather looking at him. He stared at her then waved. Heather pulled her gaze away and slunk down in her seat. Oh no, had he seen through her disguise? Did he know who she really was? She looked over to him again and her heart nearly stopped. He was walking towards the car!

'Dad, hurry up!' pleaded Heather silently. But Dad didn't come.

The lad stopped by the car. He smiled in at her. He was really good looking. Heather cautiously opened the window. Perhaps he just wanted directions or something.

'Hi!' he grinned at her. 'I'm Robbie.'

'Hi!' Heather managed a weak smile back. 'I'm, er, Emma.'

'Hey, do you live around here, Emma?' he asked.

Oh no, thought Heather. He's onto us. 'Um, no, we're just on our way to my aunt's in the city,' she fibbed, fiddling with her chin to try and cover some of her face up. 'My uncle's driving me up.' She mustn't refer to her father and arouse Robbie's suspicions.

'Oh, pity,' sighed the lad, ' 'cos I hoped I might get to see you again. You've got lovely hair, you know,' he added, shyly.

Heather smiled. 'Thanks. Thanks very much.' Good old mahogany hair dye, she thought.

Just then, Ray came out of the shop.

'Oh, here's my uncle,' said Heather, trying not to sound too relieved – or too much of a liar.

'Uh-oh, time I left then,' grinned Robbie. 'Look, here's my phone number.' He quickly scribbled a number on a chewing gum wrapper. 'Maybe you could call me? I could get into the city to see you sometime.'

'I'd like that,' said Heather, realising that she would. 'I'll try and call.'

'Bye, Emma,' said Robbie and hurried away just as Ray came up. He raised an eyebrow. Heather blushed.

'An admirer?' he asked.

'Of course!' teased Heather. 'His name's Robbie and he likes my hair.'

'Yes, I knew I shouldn't have approved of your new look,' smiled her father. 'Just don't go attracting any police officers, please!'

He put a bag of shopping on the back seat.

'What did you get?' asked Heather curiously.

'Lots of marzipan,' he told her.

'Whatever for?'

'You'll see.' He was back to being mysterious. Heather didn't pursue the matter. He would tell her when he was ready. And anyway, Heather was quite happy to sit and think about Robbie for a while.

It wasn't long before they got closer to the centre of the city. The traffic grew more and more congested, and Ray got edgier and edgier. He chewed his lip and drummed his fingers on the steering wheel every time they came to a standstill.

'Hang in there, Dad!' said Heather, a lot more cheerily than she felt.

He managed to force a smile in reply.

'Nearly there,' he said a few minutes later. 'If I've remembered my way around correctly then Marcus's office is in this next street on our left.' Ray turned smartly in front of a bus which hooted loudly.

'Yes, this is the street, Oakley Street, and there are even a few parking places left. Maybe our luck is in, after all.'

' 'Course it is, Dad,' Heather reassured him. 'Will I come in with you?'

'You'd better. We're safer if we stick together. And who knows, perhaps you'll get a cup of tea and some biscuits!'

'In that case, just stop me coming with you!' she joked.

They parked and walked to the doorway of the building. Ray pressed the buzzer and a tinny voice floated out from the intercom device asking who was calling.

'Software Solutions for Marcus – and it's very, very urgent,' Ray snapped at the machine. Heather noticed that he gave his company name, rather than his own.

It seemed an age before a whirr and a click announced that the door was open. They went inside.

Someone, presumably Marcus, was trotting down the stairs to meet them. He was a tall, good looking man, Heather noted, and very smartly dressed.

'Hello, Mr, er, Murphy!' Marcus just stopped himself in time from saying Ray's name in front of the receptionist. 'And Helen too!'

Wow! thought Heather to herself. This Marcus is sharp.

'You'd better come straight up. Cindy, no calls for the next half hour.' With that instruction to the receptionist, Marcus turned and led them up to his office. He locked the door behind them.

'I heard the radio this morning,' he admitted. 'What's going on, Ray?'

Ray paced up and down and quietly brought Marcus up to date with recent events.

'Domination got Susan McCarthy, Marcus, and they're after us now. We don't have much time. We've just got to get someone influential to listen and take up our cause, otherwise the world's in a lot of trouble.' He concluded his account and flopped exhausted into a chair.

'What a tale!' exclaimed Marcus. 'Let's see your evidence, Ray.'

Ray passed a CD to Marcus who slotted it into the drive in his computer. Ray went and looked over Marcus's shoulder.

'So this is where you found the back door?' observed Marcus as streams of data filled the screen.

'That's right,' nodded Ray. 'That's where I found the virus. Domination's software was a Trojan horse.' He jabbed a finger at certain rows of coding. 'Now, if I run the program on my laptop,' he pulled it out as he spoke, 'you'll be able to see how much further things have gone. This will be happening in every single computer that has Domination software. At my reckoning, that must be about 99% of all computers.'

'And can you stop it?' demanded Marcus.

'Yes,' said Ray triumphantly. 'But the longer it stays on a system, the more damage it does and the longer it takes to correct. We've got to move quickly.'

'Well done, Ray. I'll do anything I can to help. But what are we going to do about the police? They're a bit of a fly in the ointment aren't they?'

'That's one way of describing them I suppose!' laughed Ray. 'Look, Marcus, I can't stay here. I'd only get you into trouble for harbouring a villain. I'll leave you one set of my CDs. Can you make as many copies of them as possible for the moment, and get ready to distribute them? I've got to call on Zeus. Can you help me there too? Could you fax something through to the MD saying my software works?'

'When? Now?' asked Marcus.

'No, it would be better when I'm there myself. Can you lend me your mobile phone? I don't want to use my own in case it's being intercepted by Domination. I'll call you when I need your endorsement. And if I don't call, well, you'll know the police got there first so it'll all be over to you. Now, just one last request, can I use the bathroom please?'

'Of course, it's just down the hall,' Marcus unlocked the door. Heather noticed that Ray took his sports bag with him.

Heather, disappointed at not being offered tea and biscuits, watched silently as Marcus began making copies of her father's CDs. He flashed a smile but was too engrossed in what he was doing to talk to her.

Ray was ages. Heather was just starting to get worried when he reappeared, looking, Heather thought, a bit plumper than he had been when he went. Marcus shook his hand warmly and wished them both good luck as they left the office. Heather felt very pleased that Marcus was so supportive. But Ray still looked very grim.

'We're not out of the woods yet,' he observed. 'Zeus is going to make or break us.'

Ray felt too nervous to drive and so they flagged down a taxi which took them across the city to the plush head office of Zeus Communications. Heather sniffed a few times in the taxi.

'There's a really nice smell,' she whispered. 'Sort of almondy. Can you smell it?'

Ray nodded. 'I certainly can,' he replied.

As they pulled up outside Zeus, Ray paid the driver and they climbed out of the taxi. Heather stared up at the huge building before them. 'Awesome!'

But Ray wasn't in a mood to admire the sight. 'Come on, in we go.'

Heather could still smell that almondy smell. It must have got on their clothes and hair during the taxi ride, she guessed. Tentatively they pushed their way through the heavy revolving door and entered the air-conditioned luxury of Zeus Tower. Ray smoothed his hair down as he approached the large reception desk beside a fountain. Heather looked up. The building was designed so that it was hollow in the centre. You could see each floor with white marble railings around the central space. Heather couldn't guess how many floors there were. It was weird looking up and seeing the sides apparently closing in the higher the building went. Heather saw a few people busily coming and going at various levels above her.

'Hello, may I help you?' oozed the receptionist.

'Um, I'd like to see Mr Montgomery, please,' Ray said as assertively as he could.

'Mr Montgomery? Do you have an appointment?' The receptionist knew jolly well he didn't.

'No, I don't,' admitted Ray. 'But it is extremely urgent that I see him as soon as possible.'

The receptionist pretended to look at the diary in front of her. 'I'm afraid I can't fit you in this week. Perhaps you'd like to write to Mr Montgomery about the matter that's bothering you,' she simpered.

That was too much for Ray.

'It's not about something that's simply *bothering* me!' he exploded. 'Zeus Communications – and the whole of society – is facing ruin in the very near future. I must speak to Mr Montgomery *now*.'

With that, Ray tore open his jacket. Heather gasped almost as loudly as the receptionist. Strapped to his chest were thin rolls of a yellow substance with wires protruding from each end. He flourished a small black electronic device with a flashing red light in his hand. Heather thought it looked suspiciously like the remote control for their television.

'I'm a desperate man,' Ray shouted fiercely. 'This is dynamite. If Mr Montgomery won't see me, I'll detonate the stuff. I'll take most of the building with me. I've got nothing to lose.'

Heather was dumbstruck. Was it really dynamite her father was wearing? Or was it the marzipan he'd bought this morning? That would explain the almondy smell in the taxi! He must have rigged himself up in the toilets at Marcus's office. Wow, her dad was quite a guy!

'I'll, um, I'll see what I can do,' said the white-faced receptionist. She must have pressed some kind of silent alarm because Heather became aware of several security guards hurrying into the reception area. Ray saw them too. Then, for some reason, they both glanced up. Two floors above them, a balding, distinguished looking person was watching them.

'That's him!' Ray hissed to Heather. 'That's Lucien Montgomery – Mr Zeus himself!' In a louder voice he called 'Stay back' to the security men, whirling round to face them. Unfortunately, he whirled a bit too fast and tripped on one of his shoelaces. He crashed to the floor. Heather saw the security guards throw themselves down and cover their heads. Heather felt herself wincing too, waiting for an explosion, although she knew one wouldn't come.

Ray scrambled to his feet. The rolls of marzipan on his chest were completely flattened. Some had been squashed onto his face and neck. He looked ridiculous! Poor Ray! But suddenly Heather pulled herself together. The security guards were looking up. They were working out that this wasn't dynamite after all. Heather knew she and her father had to move quickly.

'Run, Dad, run!' she screamed, and she grabbed him and dragged him towards the door. The guards leapt up too and hurled themselves after them. But Ray and Heather had a few seconds' lead, just enough to get them to the revolving doors first. Ray paused for an instant, and looked up to where Lucien Montgomery had been standing. He was probably flat on the floor at the moment, like most of the staff. 'Montgomery, be at Instinctive Software at midday. Zeus is in real danger! I can prove it!' he roared. Then he lunged at the revolving door, pulling Heather through with him. Once they were through, Heather tore off one of her runners and threw it down so that it jammed the massive door. She looked back to see two security guards heaving at it with all their might. But the shoe was doing the trick and trapping them inside.

Heather and Ray ran for all they were worth. They got some funny looks from passers-by but no one tried to stop them. They ducked into a shopping mall. Ray rummaged for Marcus's phone in his pocket. He dialled Marcus's number.

'It's me, Ray,' he panted. 'I didn't get to see Montgomery, everything went wrong. But send him your fax. Say I was the guy who caused the commotion. I want to see him at your office at midday. Tell him you've seen that I'm right – that Domination are out to bring civilisation to its knees. Please, Marcus.'

Ray turned the phone off. He sighed. 'I really messed up, didn't I?'

'Oh, Dad,' began Heather, meaning to reassure him. But the image of him splattered with marzipan, picking himself up off the floor sprung into her mind again. She began to giggle.

'Oh, I'm sorry, Dad!' She tried to pull a straight face. 'It's just that, just that . . . ' but she couldn't control herself. The day's tensions found a release and she began to laugh out loud. Suddenly Ray joined in. He could see the funny side too. They laughed so much they had to prop each other up and wipe the tears from their eyes. They got more funny looks but then they were beginning to get used to those. Eventually, sanity took a hold again.

'Let's get a coffee,' suggested Ray. 'We've got an hour before we need to be at Marcus's again. I only hope Montgomery turns up. If he doesn't, there's nothing else we can possibly do. I shall just have to turn myself in.'

'He'll come, Dad, I'm sure he will,' said Heather, trying to believe it herself. 'But coffee would be good. Look, there's a coffee bar over there. Oh, you'd better go and clean yourself up. You've got some yellow splodges on your neck! And if you'll give me some money, I'll nip into that shoe shop over there and get myself a pair of cheap runners.'

'Goodness, I'd forgotten you were down to one shoe. And have I really got marzipan on my face? OK then, I'll see you at the coffee bar in five minutes.'

Ray disappeared off to the gents. Heather bought some canvas sneakers and wandered to the coffee bar. She chose four of the sickliest looking muffins they had, and ordered two double cappucinos. She took the heavy tray to a corner table. Dad soon joined her, looking clean again.

They idly watched the passers-by as they ate and drank. Then suddenly Heather became aware that they were being watched. She felt a prickling at the back of her neck. She casually glanced round. A few tables away, two people were sitting, apparently minding their own business. But they weren't ordinary people. The man must have been about six foot tall, blonde, blue eyes and immaculately turned out in some sort of designer suit. The woman, too, was stunning. She had a beautiful figure and wore a fantastic trouser suit. The perfect couple, thought Heather idly. Suddenly she stiffened. Perfect! That was it! She thought back to the photos of perfect people her father had collected when he was researching Domination. Her blood ran cold. These people were too perfect. They were Domination perfect!

She glanced away again. This time her eye was caught by a tall, handsome man apparently window shopping a little further down the mall. Beyond him was another perfect guy, trying to look inconspicuous reading a newspaper.

Domination had found them!

'Don't look now, Dad,' said Heather quietly, trying to swallow her fear, 'but there are some Domination people around. At the table behind us and two more in the mall.'

Ray almost dropped his cup in alarm. 'What?' he hissed. He checked out Heather's observation. He went very pale. 'That's them all right. We're trapped.'

'Stay cool, Dad. Goodness knows how they tracked us down here. But never mind that now. We can run for it, I reckon,' Heather was beginning to make plans.

'We can try,' he said, but without much hope. 'Look, I'll slide you a set of CDs under the table. If we get separated or anything, take these to show Montgomery on your own, OK?'

'OK, Dad.'

Ray fumbled as inconspicuously as possible in his bag and pushed something under the table towards Heather with his foot. Heather carelessly leant down, on the pretext of adjusting her sock, and slipped the CDs in under her jacket.

'Fancy a refill, Dad?' she said in a loud voice.

Ray looked puzzled for a moment. He was about to say that he'd had enough caffeine for now, but Heather winked at him. 'Get ready to run,' she hissed. 'I'll slow Mr and Mrs Perfect here down for us.'

'Actually, yes, more coffee would be lovely,' said Dad, nice and loudly.

Heather walked up to the counter, passing close to the Domination people. She didn't look at them, but she could feel their eyes on her.

'Two large black coffees, please.'

The counter assistant handed them over. Heather began to walk back with a mug in each hand. She saw her father poised for taking off. She came to Domination's table. She paused by it. The man and woman looked up at her, intently.

'Here, the coffee's on me!' she cried and flung the scalding coffee all over them. Pandemonium broke out. The Domination pair leapt up, shouting in pain. Heather had the presence of mind to tip the table over on them too, knocking them down before she took to her heels with Ray. The counter staff began yelling. Out of the corner of her eye, Heather saw the two lurking Domination members in the mall start to run after them.

But she and Ray had a good few metres' start. If they could just get out of the mall, they'd be able to lose themselves in the crowd outside. The door wasn't far. But then disaster struck. Ray's shoelace, cause of the fiasco at Zeus Tower, had unravelled again, and once more sent him flying. He landed very heavily. Heather stopped and turned back to help him, but Ray roared at her.

'No, go on, you're our last hope, Heather. Do it, honey!'

For a fraction of a second, Heather hesitated, uncertain what to do. She didn't like to leave her father, but the Domination guys were almost on them. He was right – she had to go. So with a last despairing look at her father, she turned and fled.

She didn't stop running for at least five minutes. She barged her way through the shoppers, who grumbled complaints – and worse – at her. She wove in and out of the crowd until at last she just had to pause for breath. She chose a busy corner, close to a flower stall, to stop and take stock.

There was no sign of Domination, thank goodness. But no sign of her father either. They must have got him, like they'd got poor Susan. Heather tried to shut her mind to what might be happening to him. Right now she had to concentrate on getting to Marcus's office. She could just about remember the address, but she wasn't sure which direction to go in. She'd ask for directions when she got her breath back. She was comforted by the bulge under her jacket. Clever of her dad to give her a set of the disks to show that Zeus guy! *If* he turned up. But Heather had a feeling that he would. She glanced at her watch. Eleven thirty. She had to hurry.

She soon found out where Oakley Street was. She jogged along, her mind in a whirl. What really bothered her was how Domination had found them in that café. They must have followed her and Dad from Zeus Tower. But how had they known they were going to Zeus in the first place? The only person who knew about that was – Marcus! Heather slowed to a walk. Oh no! Marcus must be a Domination guy! Come to think of it, he was tall and good looking, and very well dressed – the Domination trademark. So he'd been a traitor all along.

It was now five to twelve. Heather suddenly quickened her step. She had to get to Oakley Street before Montgomery arrived. The meeting Ray had set up would now be a trap. Domination would get her and Montgomery at the same time. They'd probably try to convince Montgomery that Ray was a lunatic or they'd brainwash him, or make him disappear like Susan. For a moment Heather wondered if she could trust even Lucien Montgomery. But, with a chuckle, she realised that the plump balding figure she'd seen back at Zeus Tower couldn't possibly be a Domination member. He was too ugly! She was just beginning to wonder how come all Domination people were so perfect looking when she found herself at the top of the street. One minute to go.

Oakley Street was quiet and Heather felt very conspicuous. What if Domination got to her before she got to Montgomery? She shuddered, but decided to take the risk. She began to walk resolutely down the street. At the far end, a tall, athletic figure began briskly walking towards her. Heather's legs felt weak. Hurry up, Mr Montgomery, she thought angrily. Industry moguls should know how to be punctual, surely.

She was almost at Marcus's office now. The approaching figure was quickening his stride too. Heather glanced desperately behind her. At that instant, a sleek, black limousine purred round the corner and began to drive towards her. But was this Montgomery? Or was it Domination? Then Heather saw a small flag on the bonnet. It was bright turquoise, the colour of Zeus's logo. Thank Heavens! Montgomery had come.

She ran towards the car, waving her arms. It slowed cautiously.

'Let me in!' screamed Heather through the dark,

toughened glass. 'Let me in before Domination get me!'

And Domination were after her. The original character was sprinting towards her, and two other people were hurrying down the steps outside Marcus's office. Mercifully, Mr Montgomery pushed the door open, and Heather leapt inside.

'Thanks!' she panted. Mr Montgomery smiled at her.

'Driver, get us out of here – fast!' Lucien Montgomery ordered.

The car suddenly shot forward with such power that Heather was thrown back in her seat.

'Wow!' she gasped.

'Sorry, young lady,' smiled Montgomery. 'Lucien Montgomery, as you know.' He introduced himself, holding out a hand.

Heather shook it gratefully. An ally at last. 'Heather Mayhew, as you know, I dare say!'

She managed to grin.

'Yes, we had worked out who you were,' admitted Montgomery.

'Dad wasn't really going to blow up your tower,' Heather quickly explained. 'It was only marzipan.'

'I guessed as much,' replied Montgomery. 'He seemed a desperate man. That's why I thought I'd keep this rendezvous.'

'Thank goodness you did,' agreed Heather, 'or they'd have got me too.'

'Are we being followed, driver?' enquired Montgomery, peering into the rear view mirror. Heather saw a large silver saloon reflected in it.

'Yes, sir, I rather think we are,' observed the driver.

'Try and lose them,' ordered Montgomery. He turned to Heather. 'Now, Miss Mayhew, perhaps you'd care to tell me all that's been happening.'

Heather launched into the story of how over a year ago Domination had ruined her father's business by offering their anti-hacking software free, and how since then Ray had been studying their software and spotted what it was actually doing. She explained how no one had listened to him.

'I wonder if he contacted me at the time?' mused Montgomery. 'I certainly never heard anything. If I find out that he did and that someone suppressed the information, heads will roll.'

Heather believed him. He was an awe-inspiring figure.

She went on with her tale, telling him about Susan and about the shadow she'd seen. She even told him about dyeing their hair! She finished with a brief résumé of the day's events since they'd left Zeus Tower.

'Here are Dad's CDs.' She dug the precious package out of her jacket. 'This is the only set left. Domination have got their hands on all the others. These CDs prove everything Dad claims is true. His antidote program to fight the Trojan horse is there too. Please,

Mr Montgomery, you must believe me. Dad is right. Domination will bring the world to its knees.'

'That's domination indeed!' said Montgomery, grimly. He took the CDs.

'Now for some clever tricks,' he smiled at her. He reached to his right and pulled a folding table from the side of the car. Then he lifted the tiniest laptop computer that Heather had ever seen onto it. He prompted it into life with the command, 'Computer on.' The screen lit up, presenting an array of icons. Heather watched, amazed. This was real James Bond stuff! Montgomery slid the first CD into the drive. 'Computer, virus scan and activate,' he commanded. The computer did just what it was told. Montgomery saw Heather's open mouth.

'Impressive, eh?' he chuckled. 'But one day, everyone will have computers like this. The computer mouse is a thing of the past.'

Montgomery turned back to the computer. 'Computer, email contents of CD to Z-ops.' He turned to Heather. 'They're my technical crew,' he explained. Then he went through the same operation with the other two CDs.

'Excuse me for a moment, I need to make a few calls,' he said politely to Heather. Then he flicked open his watch to reveal a miniature cell phone. He pressed a couple of buttons, and began speaking urgently and quietly. Heather strained her ears. She caught the odd word like 'Domination', 'virus' and her father's name. He made three calls in all. He snapped the phone shut.

At that moment, the computer buzzed and a message popped onto the screen.

```
Domination virus confirmed.
Immediate action required.
Disastrous scenario.
```

Montgomery was back on the phone at once. Eventually he stopped talking and turned to Heather.

'Your father is a genius, plain and simple,' he told her. 'My team are introducing his antidote program to our computer systems, and sending warnings round the world, even as I speak. Now, you have my solemn promise that your father will be recompensed in full for his work.'

'But we need to find him first,' Heather pointed out, suddenly overcome. The tears began streaming down her face. 'Please find my dad,' she begged.

Montgomery passed her a large, white silk handkerchief. Heather blew her nose noisily.

'A search is already underway. My first phone call was to the police. I'd forewarned a couple of my contacts in the force after your father's visit this morning. Some special agents were tailing him, so if Domination did get him, as you fear, the agents will have followed them. Don't worry, they'll get him back.'

Heather hoped so with all her heart.

'Driver, have we lost our company?' Montgomery asked.

'Yes, sir. The saloon was pulled over by the police about five minutes ago.'

'Excellent,' said Montgomery. Heather had to agree.

'Ah,' he said, a few minutes later, looking out through the window. 'Home.' Zeus Tower loomed above them.

As they drew up, Heather saw a crowd of people gathered outside. Some of them turned, saw the car and charged towards it. There were some bright flashes.

'My goodness,' observed Montgomery dryly. 'News travels fast. Our friends the press are here.'

'Do they know about Domination already?' gasped Heather.

'Don't forget, Miss Mayhew, I *am* the head of Zeus Communications. Communicating is what we are all about!' Montgomery smiled.

Heather managed to smile back although she was still worried sick about her father. She'd been encouraged by what Montgomery had said about the special agents, but that didn't guarantee his safety.

'We'll have to run for the door, I'm afraid,' sighed Montgomery. 'My security men will keep the media hounds off us.'

Heather looked out through the window and recognised the guards she'd last seen hammering on the revolving door, trying to catch her and her father earlier that morning. She felt a smug sense of satisfaction at having outwitted them with her shoe! They obviously bore no grudges and sheltered her and Montgomery as they battled through the journalists into the building and then held the mob at bay. Heather sighed with relief. She was about to turn to Montgomery, to ask what would happen now, when a familiar voice rang out from above her.

'Heather! Oh Heather, honey!'

'Dad!' she cried back, unable to believe her ears. She looked up and saw her father's face looking down at her from the second floor.

'Where are the stairs?' she yelled, looking about her so she could rush up them and hug him.

'Behind that door,' someone pointed, and Heather was through it like a streak of lightning. She hurtled up the stairs, three at a time. She heard someone hurtling down towards her. She turned a corner on the first floor – and there was her dad! He had broken glasses and a black eye, but apart from that he looked fine. Heather threw herself into his arms and began to sob uncontrollably. They clung to one another, each reunited with the most precious thing on earth.

'Um, excuse me, would you like to come to Mr Montgomery's suite?' a voice gently enquired, an eternity later.

Heather and Ray looked up. It was Mr

Montgomery's receptionist. 'The police are waiting there. It seems they have some good news!' she beamed.

'Hopefully that means they're going to drop all charges against me,' smiled Ray. 'Oh, Heather, thank heavens you're safe. You must tell me everything I missed. You obviously saved the day. Oh my clever girl!' He hugged her again.

'And what happened to you?' gushed Heather. 'I was sure Domination would get you. I thought I'd never see you again.' That was the wrong thing to say, because the tears started again. She wiped them away quickly. They began to follow the receptionist up the white stairs.

'Well, after you left me flat on my face, I got up ready to run again, but one of the Domination guys grabbed me. Then next thing I knew, two other chaps had dashed up and began laying into the Domination thugs.'

'They were special agents,' Heather informed him. 'Mr Montgomery had them sent after you.'

'Yes, so I discovered later,' said Ray. 'Anyway, there was quite a fight – lots of martial arts stuff. I got caught in the crossfire.' He fingered his purple, puffy eye gingerly.

'Oh, poor Dad!'

'Anyway, the agents won the day and whisked me off to a waiting car. Goodness, I sound just like a spy novel, don't I? I didn't see what happened to the

Domination pair. One minute they were lying on the floor, but when I looked back, they'd just gone. Vanished!'

'Good, so long as they're not still around,' said Heather firmly. 'And the agents brought you here, then?'

'Yes, to wait for Montgomery to come back with you – as we all hoped. Oh, I was so worried about you! Especially after I realised that Marcus was a traitor.'

'Yes, I worked that one out too,' said Heather. 'I wonder if the police have got him?'

'Maybe that's the good news,' said Ray. 'Anyway, here's Montgomery's office so we'll find out now.'

So they were ushered into the office. And what a suite it was. The main room was enormous. To one side was a huge, polished oak table, surrounded by about twenty plush chairs. Across from that was a gleaming white marble desk with an array of white and turquoise leather armchairs in front of it. Montgomery sat regally behind his desk. Two police officers sat in armchairs.

'What's the good news we heard about?' asked Ray, anxiously.

'We've found Miss McCarthy,' replied one of the police officers.

'Brilliant!' cried Heather.

'Is she all right?' asked Ray.

'Tired and stressed, but otherwise fine. They're

keeping her in hospital overnight for observation. We'll be interviewing her presently. We found her in the car that was chasing Mr Montgomery. But that's the strangest thing. My boys pulled the car over while it was in pursuit. But when they opened the doors, it was completely empty, except for Miss McCarthy. She claims that they just, um, sort of vanished from in front of her eyes.' The police officer obviously felt a bit silly saying that. 'But the evidence from my people who apprehended the vehicle supports that claim. They clearly saw persons in the car when they stopped it, but then they apparently disappeared into thin air.'

'So Domination weren't human, then,' faltered Heather.

Everyone turned to look at her.

'Well, they can't have been,' she went on, more confidently. 'Don't you remember, Dad, that first announcement that came up on your email the day Domination launched its software? The strange wording? It was something along the lines of "our program will deal with the problems that threaten your world" or something like that.'

'Good grief, that's right!' Ray stood up in excitement. 'I just thought it was a bad translation from another language. But maybe not.'

'And remember how no one could find out much about Domination or where they'd come from? The company just seemed to appear from nowhere, didn't it? And all the people were so perfect looking – they were just too perfect to be real!'

'That's right,' he agreed. 'Presumably Domination was the front for some sort of life force that wanted to dominate Earth. Look, the name gives it away! Maybe they'd studied us for a while and saw that modern technology and the problems of hacking and computer viruses offered the ideal opportunity for their purposes. If they could throw the world into chaos with their software – incapacitate our satellites and disable early warning systems and so on – they could invade or infiltrate or whatever the heck aliens do. Heather, you've cracked it!'

The police officers didn't look quite so convinced. 'We will be pursuing our enquiries,' said one of them, a touch stiffly. 'We need to interview you too, Mr Mayhew.'

'Yes, I rather thought you might,' sighed Ray. 'No time like the present, I suppose.'

'You can use my boardroom for some privacy,' suggested Montgomery. 'I'll get my secretary to take you there.'

'Will Dad go to prison?' asked Heather anxiously after her father had gone.

'Whatever for?' asked Mr Montgomery, in surprise.

'Well, he used false number plates on our car so we could give Domination the slip for a while, and he scared everyone in your building when he pretended he had dynamite on him!' Heather reeled off his crimes.

'I have no intention of pressing charges for that!' laughed Montgomery. 'Your father was trying to save us all – and he has. His brilliant new program has halted the damage Domination's so-called anti-hacking software was doing. My Z-ops team tell me his program is absolutely foolproof. They've never seen such impressive software engineering, they said. I shall be asking your father to head up Z-ops while they work on disseminating his anti-virus program over the Web and in whatever other media are necessary.'

'Wow, Dad a Z-op!' exclaimed Heather. Wait till her friends heard about this!

'And you're a famous young lady, too. You'll be all over the papers and the news tonight. I know that all the major news companies of the world want to interview you. As soon as you feel up to it, I'll arrange a venue.'

'I'd better wait for Dad,' said Heather, nervously. Then suddenly she thought of something. 'Can I make a phone call, please?'

Montgomery handed her a turquoise cell phone and busied himself with some papers on his desk. Heather dug Robbie's phone number out of her pocket and dialled. The answer-phone came on.

Heather cleared her throat. 'Hi Robbie, it's Emma, only I'm really Heather – Heather Mayhew. You'll see me on the news tonight. I had to lie to you because we were running away from Domination and the police, but it's OK, we're not criminals,' she added quickly. 'I'm sorry I lied. And my hair's dyed. But I hope you still want to see me some time. I . . . um . . . I think you're very nice. I'll call again soon. Bye.'

She felt herself blushing. Mr Montgomery pretended not to have heard.

Ray and the police officers came back into the room. Ray looked relieved and Heather noticed he wasn't in handcuffs.

'I got off with a caution,' he told her, 'seeing as how I've saved the world!' He grinned.

Mr Montgomery got all business-like and discussed contracts and royalties and things with Ray, who looked a bit pale at some of the figures Montgomery was mentioning. In the end Ray agreed to head up Z-ops for the Domination Decontamination Project, as Mr Montgomery called it. Then the head of Zeus sent them up to an apartment at the top of the tower to rest and change – someone had already gone out to buy them new outfits – while he organised a press conference.

At last they were left to themselves.

Friday 31 December 2004

Ten minutes to go till midnight. Heather escaped from the noise and excitement in the lounge where Ray's New Year's party was in full swing and, pulling her jacket on, went outside into the cold night air. It was a beautiful night – bitingly cold but clear and dry. A million stars sparkled. What a high note to end such an exciting year on, thought Heather.

She looked back at the house. Ray was close to being a millionaire now, thanks to his brilliant software package – and to Zeus, of course. They'd just moved to another big, old house, not far from their first home. Ray commuted up to Zeus Tower three days a week now, and ran his own computer consultancy the other two. Heather's life went on much as before, only with a bit more luxury. Her hair was still mahogany!

'Hey, are you running away from me?' came a voice. It was Robbie. He'd come to the party as Heather's special guest. They'd been out many times since April. It wasn't very easy with them being so far apart but they both enjoyed each other's company enough to make it all worthwhile.

' 'Course not,' smiled Heather. 'I just needed some fresh air, and since Auntie Jane had you pinned to the wall, I came out on my own!'

'She was just trying to find out whether I'm worthy of you!' laughed Robbie. 'Anyway, you'd better come on in. There's only a couple of minutes to go till we all join hands and sing and stuff.'

Heather and Robbie hurried inside, hand in hand. They bumped into Susan McCarthy.

'Hi, you runaways!' she grinned. Heather wasn't the only one who had found romance thanks to Domination. Susan and Ray had become very close over the last eight months. Heather had been jealous at first – for so long she'd had her father to herself. But she liked Susan and was getting used to the idea of having her around.

'Heather, your father sent me to look for you,' said Susan. 'He wants everyone here for the countdown to the New Year. Come on, quickly!'

'OK, Sue!' replied Heather.

' . . . fifteen, fourteen . . . ' the countdown had begun. Heather, Robbie and Susan joined in, grabbing hands.

' . . . ten, nine, eight, seven, six, five, four, three, two, one, Happy New Year!'

A Domination-free New Year.